T0365346

Patches

Written by Earl Irvin
Illustrated by Raynald Kudemus

Print information available on the last page

Rev. date: 03/09/2016

To order additional copies of this book, contact:
Xlibris
1-888-795-4274
www.Xlibris.com
Orders@Xlibris.com

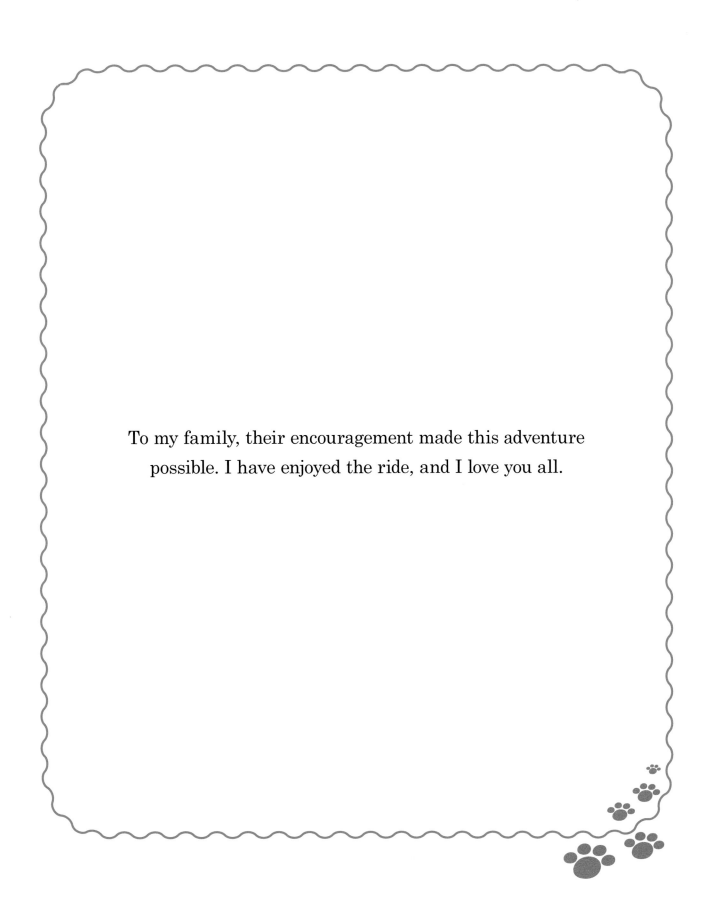

To my family, their encouragement made this adventure possible. I have enjoyed the ride, and I love you all.

Hello. My name is Patches, and this is my story. I was born in Henderson, Arkansas. I have five siblings. My human family has three children: Earl, Mike, and Marie. Marie is a girl, and she is the youngest. She ran and played like she is one of the boys. We lived on a farm with pigs, cows, and horses. We loved to play in the sunshine. I had never been off the back porch.

One day something interesting happened. When I was about two months old, Earl said, "We are going to Florida to visit Nanny and Pampa."

The next morning, Mike took me from my box before daylight, and we got into the van. Everyone was excited! I was so thrilled that I did not even realize that none of my brothers or sisters was with us. I was so lucky to be the only one in my family who is going to see Nanny and Pampa.

The boys were talking about all the things we were going to do in Florida. Mike called it a vacation. It sure sounded like fun. When we get home, I will tell my brothers and sisters all about my vacation.

We traveled for a long time before we arrived in Florida. I ate two times along the way. My human family brought my bowl for me. When they ate, they threw away their dishes. I always had my own little bowl with a place for food and a place for water.

Every time I would wake up from napping, someone different was sleeping, and someone else was watching the picture box. They called that a video.

Nanny and Pampa lived in the woods. As we approached the house, Marie held me up so that I could look out of the window. All I could see were tall, skinny trees. It was dark outside. I knew there would be no playing, even if Nanny and Pampa had a porch like ours. I did not know if I was going to enjoy my vacation.

I never saw trees like this at home. I heard sounds that I had never heard. Marie said, "Don't worry, those are just crickets." I will avoid crickets. They made such loud noises. Crickets must be really big, or there must be an awful lot of them. When I get home, I am going to tell my brothers and sisters about crickets.

Pampa's place was not like our farm. There were no other people or animals as far as I could see. All they had were trees and crickets.

I did not want to get out of the van. I began to shiver, and it wasn't even cold. Earl stroked my back and tickled me under my chin. He said, "It's OK, you will like it here. Wait until you meet Nanny and Pampa." I did not want him to let me go. I snuggled myself into his arms, as closely as I could get.

At home, I always slept outside with my mother, brothers, and sisters in a small box. We all tried to sleep next to Mother to stay warm. I did not see a box on the porch. Where was I going to sleep?

That night, I slept with Marie. Nanny was not happy. Pampa said, "He probably needs a couple of days to get used to us." This was my first time to sleep inside a house, and my first time to sleep on a bed. The bed was large and soft. The boys slept in another bed in the same room. I could get used to sleeping in a big, soft bed.

One day after breakfast, my human family packed up our things and loaded the van. That was not too bad for a vacation. I slept inside with my human family. I slept in a big, soft bed. I ate the same kind of food that I had eaten at home. And I did not see any of those crickets that I heard on the night we arrived.

We were going home, and Nanny and Pampa were going with us. They probably did not like those crickets either. It sure seemed like everyone was in an awfully big hurry to leave.

I had just curled up between two pillows in the back of the van for a short nap when we stopped. Everyone jumped out of the van, and the boys began yelling. What was happening? They were making so much noise. I just knew one of those crickets must have gotten into the van with us.

There were no crickets. There were no trees. Everywhere I looked, there was water. This was nothing like the puddle by the porch at home. This was huge! The dirt looked different too. All I could see was water and the pale dirt.

Marie picked me up and walked in the direction of the water. Did I mention that I did not like water? I tried to get away from her. She was confused. "This is the beach," she said as she held me tightly, "and this is sand."

I wondered how many kittens could drink from a bowl this big and not see one another. I knew that I would never see this much water in one place again.

Marie put me in a small cage that was sitting on a blanket. I felt a misty rain on my coat. I already told you that I did not like getting wet! I tried to clean myself. As I licked my fur, I had a strange sensation. This did not taste like the water at home. The sand did not feel like the dirt at home. Pampa said this was saltwater.

The sand and the heat made me tired. I slept. I began to dream about the beach and all that water. I dreamed that I was alone at the beach. This was something else to tell my brothers and sisters about when I got home—the crickets, a bed, and the beach with all the water and sand.

That night Pampa gave me some shrimp, oysters, and crabmeat. The taste reminded me of my regular food, but the texture was different. Dinner was the best that I had eaten in Florida. Pampa told me what each thing was. He made sure everything was in little pieces as he put it into my bowl. The shrimp was chunky. The crabmeat was stringy. The oysters were slippery. I did not miss my regular food. This was good. I wondered why we never ate like this at home. We sure had good food on our vacation.

Everyone in my human family and Nanny played in the water at the beach every day. While they played, Pampa and I sat on a blanket and stayed away from the water. When the water looked like it was going to get us, Pampa would get up and drag the blanket to a new spot. He would say, "Time to move, Patches, unless you want a bath." Pampa and I never went near the water, but every night I had to clean myself. That water was nasty. The only good thing about the beach was that we had shrimp, oysters, and crabmeat to eat every night.

One morning, we did not go to the beach. Everyone loaded our things into the van, and we left. At last, we were going home. I was tired of the beach. I was tired of that cage. I climbed into Earl's lap and began licking his arm. It was warmer and redder than usual. Yuck! It tasted like the water from the beach. He immediately took me off his lap and gave me to Mike. What did I do to make him mad? I licked his arms at home, and he never objected.

When I licked Mike's arm, he put me under the seat. I was confused. What happened? No one wanted to pet me. Well, that was fine with me! If they did not want me around, I would just stay under the seat all the way home! Florida sure did affect my human family strangely. I do not ever want to go to the beach again.

I curled up under the seat and fell asleep thinking about my brothers and sisters. I dreamed that I told them about the crickets, a bed, all the water and sand, seafood, and the strange ride home. Maybe they would know why my family acted so oddly.

It was still daylight when we stopped. Everyone climbed out of the van, unloading the beach things and that awful cage. I peeked from beneath the seat. We were not home. We were at Nanny and Pampa's house, again. I thought we were going home. I wanted to see my brothers and sisters. I was not getting out of the van until we got home. I tried to hide under the back seat. If they could not find me, I would not have to get out of the van.

Earl crawled into the van and reached under the rear seat. He grabbed my two front paws and pulled me out of the van. I struggled. I did not want to be here. I wanted to go home. I was tired of vacation and the beach. "It is all right," he said as he held me tightly in his arms, walking toward the house.

I was still in Florida, and there was nothing I could do about it. I would not think about the beach. I would be positive. I would think about all the good things at Pampa's. I thought about the seafood. I thought about sleeping inside the house. I thought about that big, soft bed.

We were standing at the foot of the porch when I saw the cricket! He was enormous, almost as big as one of the baby horses at home. He was red in color, and his hair was long and untidy. I bet that he never spent the entire day trying to stay pretty.

As he stood at the door, it almost looked like his fur was on fire. His tongue was huge. It hung from his mouth and down his chin. He could probably wrap his tongue around me and swallow me whole. I knew his breath smelled like a used litter box.

His teeth were jagged, like the oyster shells at the beach. He had so many of them too. I wondered how he had room for his large tongue with all those teeth in his mouth.

Mike and Marie had talked about a dinosaur in a movie that could not see you unless you moved. I whispered to myself over and over again, "If I just stay still, he will not see me. If I just stay still, he will not see me. If I just stay still . . ."

Too late! He saw me! He growled. The noise was not what I heard when we arrived in Florida. I began to scurry up Earl's arm and scratched him as I did so. He yelled for help. Pampa came around the corner of the house. He grabbed that cricket and said, "Rebel, no dawg of mine is gonna hurt a little kitten." He added, "You will get used to her. Go inside the house."

That was no cricket. That was a dog. I had seen horses and cows, but never a dog. After meeting Rebel, those crickets did not seem scary at all. What was I going to do next time I saw that dog?

We all went into the house. I played on the bed with Marie for a little while. Pampa yelled for us to come to dinner. Just as I jumped off the bed, Nanny picked me up and put me out the door and left me there—alone.

Pampa brought me my bowl filled with food and water. It was not the seafood from the beach, or the other soft food that I had eaten. The pieces were smaller than the seafood. They were hard and crunchy. When I ate the first one, it scratched against the top of my mouth. I did not like this new food. I did not like being alone on the porch.

What had I done to make Pampa so mad at me? Why did Rebel eat inside, and I had to eat on the porch? I did not like to be left alone. I did not like that dog. He was a nasty animal with a mouth full of jagged teeth. I would eat the small crunchy food, but I was definitely staying clear of that dog!

After dinner, Rebel came outside and went to the other end of the porch. He collapsed on a big pillow. This was his home. Where were his manners? I was the guest. Although he never growled at me again, he did show me a peek at his teeth. When a squirrel ran through the yard, he moved his head toward the squirrel, but he always kept one eye on me.

I knew he wanted to eat me. I could tell by the look in his eyes. He was going over the menu. Patches with rice. Patches with noodles. Patches with potatoes. Patches with anything; as long as he was eating Patches. I guess that was what Pampa meant by "getting used to me." I was not getting used to him. When I get home, I will warn my brothers and sisters about dogs.

It did not get any better. That night, I slept in the cage from the beach. I stuck one of my front paws through the wire and purred. I even produced a few tears.

Mike said, "The cage will protect you." Protect me? Oh no, I had forgotten about the crickets and the dog. I withdrew to the rear of the box. I curled up on a towel as I tried to sleep. I heard all kinds of noises that night. I was afraid. I missed the soft bed.

I awoke as Mike pulled me out of the cage. He picked me up and hugged me. It felt so good. I had made it through the night. My human family loved me again.

There was a lot of hugging and kissing that morning. Nanny hugged everyone. Everyone hugged me. Earl said apologetically, "Sorry about the ride from the beach, Patches. I had sunburn." What was sunburn? They talked about all the fun they had. They talked about the ride home. I could not get home quickly enough. Crickets. The beach. That dog. That nasty, crunchy food. And sunburn. I am not coming back to Florida again!

Pampa was the last to hug me. He held me tightly on his chest for a long time. He rubbed the length of my tail and popped it in a pulling motion. "How about it, Patches? Did you have fun?" I thought he finally liked me now that I was leaving. "Florida is not too bad, girl. You will get used to it," he said. What did he mean?

Pampa held me firmly. I turned my head slightly and saw that Nanny was crying. "They will be back soon." Pampa said. *They will be back! What does that mean?*

When he put me down, my human family was gone. I was stuck in Florida. I was scared, and I was worried. Pampa said they would be back soon. What did he mean? When would my family come back?

Nanny didn't seem worried when Pampa said soon. Maybe they were just going to the beach again. Nanny must have been crying because she wanted to go to the beach too. Everyone knew that Pampa and I did not like the salty water or the sand. *They will be back soon*, I kept telling myself. *They will be back soon, and I will be going home with them.*

At night, I slept in the cage. The dog must be used to me. After a few days, he even stopped snarling and showing me his teeth. He just watched me. I did not think he wanted to eat me anymore. When I get home, I am still going to warn my brothers and sisters about dogs and how oddly they behave.

I was getting used to this food. Rebel eats crunchy food like mine, but his was little balls. I stole a taste of it one time. It was worse than mine. All I could taste was the salt. At least mine tasted like the fish we ate at the beach. Once in a while, Pampa used the humming machine, and both Rebel and I ate soft food.

We ate in the afternoons. Pampa would sit on the porch and talk to us. He told us about when he was a little boy and a dog he had then. He told us about the sky and the different types of clouds. I liked the sound of Pampa's voice and his stories. The dog watched me, and I watched him. Some mornings I would walk to the gate with Pampa and look down the road for my other family.

A short time after my family left, these tiny critters began biting me. I could not even see them. When I began scratching myself, Nanny gave me a little white necklace to wear. She said it would protect me. Pampa said it was a flea collar.

Then, I discovered buzzers—that's what I call them. I hear them just before it gets dark. They make a constant buzzing noise. Pampa and Nanny put on all kinds of smelly stuff to keep the buzzers away from them. Otherwise, they are slapping their arms and legs. I believe Nanny called them mosquitoes. All the critters in Florida have weird names—crickets, dogs, fleas, and mosquitoes.

Every morning Pampa brings me into the house. He gives me a little bowl of milk. Even though Pampa told me it was milk, I already knew. I wonder what milk would taste like on my crunchy food. Maybe one day Pampa will give me some. I am sure it will make the crunchy food soft. It might even taste better. Pampa said that milk is good for me. He said it would make my bones strong. He knows everything.

One day, I jumped up on the counter in the bathroom. You will never believe what I saw. There was another me. The other kitten did everything I did. I tried to touch her, and she tried to touch me. I could not feel the soft spot on the bottom of her paw. I could not feel her rough tongue when I licked her.

Pampa called it a mirror. The mirror was cold and hard. I will tell my brothers and sisters about mirrors when I get home. I wonder what they will do when they see themselves. I chuckled when I thought about that.

Pampa and I spent our days together. We would walk around the yard, and he would tell me about the different kinds of flowers and trees.

When I got big enough, I started climbing the trees in Pampa's yard. It was fun to climb the trees. I saw lots of flowers from the limbs of the trees. We do not have many trees at home. There is a lot of corn, but nothing as tall as the pine trees in Florida.

Another time, I climbed a tall tree. I was so high in the tree that I could not get down again. I meowed really loudly until Pampa climbed the ladder and rescued me. He is always looking out for me.

Most days we walk around the yard together. Pampa showed me a gopher and warned me about snakes. He cautioned me about going into big bushes or running too far away from him. No matter where we went or what we did, Pampa would talk to me. He would tell me about the different kinds of plants and other small animals.

We have a garden. It has a little fence around it. I watched as Pampa put up the fence. He said it was a hog wire fence, but I never saw any hogs. He tied plastic grocery bags to the top of the fence posts. Pampa said the bags scare deer and other animals away from our garden.

When we started the garden, Pampa told me he was tilling the soil. I tried to help him, but I got dirty, and I do not like to get dirty. He put little seeds in the dirt and watered them every day.

One day after I had enjoyed my bowl of milk, we went to the garden. Everything was green, and the plants were all bigger than me. I was so excited. I jumped all around Pampa. He looked down at me and smiled. "I'm glad you are here, Patches. This is your garden too, you know."

OUR GARDEN

We would go to the garden every day. Pampa told me the smaller green balls were strawberries. He said, "When they turn red, we can eat them with ice cream." That sounded good to me. Pampa had given me ice cream once. It was sweeter than milk. I wonder what ice cream would taste like with strawberries in it.

The plants next to the strawberries were bigger. Pampa said they were tomatoes. They were soft and slippery. I grabbed a little one that was on the ground with my claws, and it squirted soft seeds and warm juice on me. These tomatoes were a lot different from strawberries.

Pampa said, "After we eat all of our strawberries and tomatoes, we will pick blueberries and blackberries." He said they grew wild, and we would pick them in a few months.

As we headed to the house that day, Pampa and I took a long glance back at the garden. I was so proud. Pampa said tilling the soil, planting seeds, watering, and weeding were a lot of work, but it was worth it. When I see my brothers and sisters, I am going to tell them all about our garden. We are growing peanuts next. I cannot wait to hear about peanuts.

I heard Pampa say this morning that it was chilly at the beach. How much fun could anyone have in cold, salty water at the beach? I hope the kids are having fun at the beach. I sure am having fun with Pampa.

When I see my brothers and sisters, I will tell them all about crickets, the beach, a dog, fleas, mosquitoes, and our garden. I will tell them about ice cream and picking blackberries. Every day is an adventure with Pampa. I have learned so much since I have been here. After all, I was only a kitten when I came to Florida.

This morning, Pampa brought a rolling box to the front of the house. He said, "This is a wheelbarrow, and today we are going to rake leaves." I wonder how different that will be from working in the garden.

There is always something to do with Pampa. He talks to me as if I could answer him. That is one of the things I really like about Pampa. Whether we are eating shrimp at the beach or working in the garden, he is always telling me something. I think Pampa just likes to talk to me.

Raking leaves is more work than working in the garden. I wanted to help Pampa. I am too small to push the wheelbarrow. When I tried to gather leaves, they got stuck in my claws, and it was difficult to get rid of them. Pampa saw me fighting with the leaves. He picked me up and removed the leaves from my claws.

He put me onto the ground. He gently scolded me, "You're making a mess, Patches. We will be here all day if I have to keep getting leaves out of your claws."

I had to find a way to help Pampa. How could I help rake leaves? Suddenly, it came to me. I knew how I could help him.

The next time Pampa put a pile of leaves into the wheelbarrow, I dove in after them. I curled my paws under my body close to my belly. I was careful not to disturb many leaves. I rolled slowly onto my back. I stretched my entire body. I moved gently around on the leaves to keep them from blowing out of the wheelbarrow. He just smiled at me. I was helping. We are a great team! There is always something to do in Florida. I am glad that I have Pampa to do it with me.